This is a story about a
Bullies pick on weaker people called

Butch is the bully and the victim is Luis.
You may know kids like Butch and Luis in
your own school.

What is a <u>bully</u>? What is a <u>victim</u>?

Copyright © 1994 James B. Boulden
It is illegal to reproduce this material.

Printed in
the USA

Please draw a face showing how you feel about bullies.

**Art by
Phil Fountain**

BOULDEN PUBLISHING
P.O. Box 1186; Weaverville, CA 96093
Phone (800)238-8433 FAX (916)623-5525

**Editor
Evelyn Mercer Ward**

One day Butch was hungry,
but didn't have any money of his own.
He hated the other kids who had
lots of good food to eat for lunch.

Butch looked for a smaller kid he could take
money away from.

What would you do if a bully tried to take your

lunch? _____

Butch saw Mary Anne,
but he knew better than to pick on her.
She had a big brother who protected her.
Butch sure didn't want to fight him.

Who can help you if a bully comes around?

Then Butch saw Slim, who looked him right in the eye and smiled.

Butch could see by the way Slim was walking so tall and proud, that he wouldn't scare easily.

How could Butch tell that Slim wasn't afraid?

Butch started toward Sara, but she began to scream for HELP when she saw him coming.

Butch didn't want anything to do with her.

Why do bullies often stay away from kids who yell for help? _____

Then Butch saw Luis hiding from him.

"Hey kid," said Butch.
"You look like you have lots to eat."

How can a bully tell if you are afraid of him?

Butch started to pick on Luis, trying to make him fight back.

Luis was too frightened to think.

What would you do if a bully picked on you?

A crowd of kids came to watch the fight. Butch felt strong and liked the attention.

Luis tried to fight back, but was hurt bad.

Why do bullies like to hurt other kids?

Luis started to cry.
Then he gave Butch his lunch money.

The other kids were laughing at Luis.
He felt awful about himself.

What do you think of Luis?

Luis had these feelings when Butch picked on him.

ANGRY	*AFRAID*	*STUPID*
EMBARRASSED	*WORTHLESS*	*HELPLESS*
HURT	*LONELY*	*WEAK*
UNLOVED	*VIOLENT*	*ASHAMED*

Circle those feelings that you have had too.

Now you know how it feels to be a victim.

Write down feelings that you think Butch had when he was hurting Luis.

_____

_____

_____

_____

Circle those feelings that you have had too.

Now you know how it feels to be a bully.

Butch told Luis that he would hurt
him again if he told anyone.

Bullies often use threats to keep grown-ups
from finding out that they hurt other kids.

Should Luis tell a grown-up? Why or why not?

The school counselor, Mr. Brown,
had seen what was going on.

He sent Butch and Luis home.
Then he called their parents.

What would happen to Butch and Luis at

your school? _____

When Luis got home, his mother gave him a piece of cake so he would feel better.

Victims often pretend to be weak so that they will be treated good.

What would your mom do if you were sent home for fighting at school?

Many bullies are also victims.

Butch's father was very angry with Butch for getting into trouble at school.

What would your dad do if you were sent home for fighting at school?

Luis went to see Mr. Brown the next day.

The counselor said that Luis acted weak and afraid, so Butch knew he would be easy to bully.

How do victims walk and talk?

Mr. Brown said that most of us have been a bully at some time. It makes us feel strong.

Luis remembered that he had kicked his puppy after Butch picked on him.

When is a time you were a bully?

Mr. Brown said that bullies sometimes use words and trickery rather than muscle to get other kids to do what they want.

Not all bullies are boys; some are girls. Butch had a sister named Bertha who was also a bully.

What is time when you were bullied?

Bullies sometimes hurt weaker kids to get even for the times someone has hurt them.

This makes the bully feel like they are better than the victim and in control.

Why do bullies want their victims to fight?

The worst hurt about being bullied was that it made Luis feel bad about himself.

He felt helpless and stupid and afraid.

How did you feel when someone bullied you ?

*D*raw a picture of yourself with a bully.

Bullies want to fight weaker kids because they know they will win.

The only way for you to win is to refuse to fight. This is not being a coward or chicken.

How would you feel about walking away from a fight? _____

Mr. Brown gave Luis a list of things he could do to keep from being picked on.

1. *Make up your mind not to be bullied.*

2. *Think ahead what to do if a bully does pick on you.*

3. *Stand up straight and walk tall.*

4. *Look other kids in the eye.*

5. *Stay away from where bullies hang out.*

6. *Treat bullies with respect.*

7. *Call for help if a bully starts trouble.*

8. *Stay calm. Don't react.*

9. *Refuse to fight.*

10. *Try talking quietly or use humor.*

11. *Walk slowly away.*

What usually happens if you fight a bully?

_____

Give two ideas for avoiding getting picked on.

1)_____

2)_____

Give two ideas for getting along with a bully.

1)_____

2)_____

_What will you say to the next bully
who bothers you?_

_____

_____

Is it all right for you to ask for help?_____

Where can you get help if you need it?_____

_____

Later, Butch came in to see Mr. Brown.

Butch had been in trouble lots of times and thought everyone was against him.

Name two bad things about being a bully.

1)_____

2)_____

Mr. Brown asked Butch if he was trying to get even for his own hurts.
Or maybe he was acting like some tough person he knew or saw in a movie.

Butch didn't want to talk about that.

Why do some people bully other people?

Mr. Brown explained there are other ways to get attention than pushing kids around.

Butch admitted that he did not have many friends.

Why don't bullies have many friends?

Mr. Brown said Butch might become a peacemaker or a mediator.

Rather than hurting other kids, Butch could help keep them from hurting each other.

What is a peacemaker or a mediator?

Peacemakers and mediators stop trouble
rather than start it.

Other kids like to be around them.
Peacemakers can be heroes.

How would you feel about being a peacemaker?

After talking with Mr. Brown, Butch and his sister both decided to be peacemakers.

They agreed to take special training to learn to do this well.

What is one advantage of being a peacemaker

B utch and Luis never did become friends, but now they respect each other.

Luis has learned how to keep other kids from picking on him and Butch has more friends.

Butch and Luis are both much happier now than when they played bully and victim.

Content Editors

We are grateful to the many professionals who contributed time and experience in the development of this publication.

Special recognition is extended to the following counselors: *Christy Reinold, Una Simental, Shelly Borchardt, Joanna Hansen, Nancy Prisk, Cherri Stefanic and Nancy Motter.*

NURTURING RESOURCES FOR ALL AGES

Bereavement ✳ *Divorce* ✳ *Remarriage* ✳ *Blended Family*
Single Parent ✳ *Feelings Awareness* ✳ *Self-Esteem*
Sexual Abuse ✳ *Physical Abuse* ✳ *Substance Abuse*
Bullying ✳ *Making Friends* ✳ *Misbehavior*

ACTIVITY BOOKS, REPRODUCIBLE WORKBOOKS, MASKS, PUPPETS, POSTERS AND DRAW-A-FACE PACKS

Used by 10,000 Counselors.
Award winning. One-half million copies in print.
High quality at a low price.

Call 800/238-8433 for a free catalog

BOULDEN PUBLISHING
P.O. Box 1186, Weaverville, CA 96093